THE WONDERFUL WIZARD OF OZ

VOL. 2

ADAPTED FROM THE NOVEL BY L. FRANK BAUM

Writer: ERIC SHANOWER
Artist: SKOTTIE YOUNG
Colorist: JEAN-FRANCOIS BEAULIEU
Letterer: JEFF ECKLEBERRY

Assistant Editors: LAUREN SANKOVITCH & LAUREN HENRY
Associate Editor: NATE COSBY
Senior Editor: RALPH MACCHIO

Special Thanks to Chris Allo, Rich Ginter, Jeff Suter & Jim Nausedas
Collection Editor: MARK D. BEAZLEY
Assistant Editors: NELSON RIBEIRO & ALEX STARBUCK
Editor, Special Projects: JENNIFER GRÜNWALD
Senior Editor, Special Projects: JEFF YOUNGQUIST
SVP of Print & Digital Publishing Sales: DAVID GABRIEL
Production: JERRY KALINOWSKI
Book Design: SPRING HOTELING

Editor in Chief: AXEL ALONSO
Chief Creative Officer: JOE QUESADA
Publisher: DAN BUCKLEY
Executive Producer: ALAN FINE

visit us at www.abdopublishing.com

Reinforced library bound edition published in 2014 by Spotlight, a division of the ABDO Group, PO Box 398166, Minneapolis, Minnesota 55439. Spotlight produces high-quality reinforced library bound editions for schools and libraries. Published by agreement with Marvel Characters, Inc.

Printed in the United States of America, North Mankato, Minnesota.
102013
012014
This book contains at least 10% recycled materials.

Marvel.com
© 2014 Marvel

Library of Congress Cataloging-in-Publication Data

Shanower, Eric.
  The wonderful Wizard of Oz / adapted from the novel by L. Frank Baum ; writer: Eric Shanower ; artist: Skottie Young. -- Reinforced library bound edition.
     pages cm
  "Marvel."
  Summary: An eight-volume, graphic novel adaptation of L. Frank Baum's tales of Dorothy, a little girl from Kansas who is blown by a storm to the magical land of Oz, where she has amazing adventures while trying to get home.
  ISBN 978-1-61479-226-0 (vol. 1) -- ISBN 978-1-61479-227-7 (vol. 2) -- ISBN 978-1-61479-228-4 (vol. 3) -- ISBN 978-1-61479-229-1 (vol. 4) -- ISBN 978-1-61479-230-7 (vol. 5) -- ISBN 978-1-61479-231-4 (vol. 6) -- ISBN 978-1-61479-232-1 (vol. 7) -- ISBN 978-1-61479-233-8 (vol. 8)
  1. Graphic novels. [1. Graphic novels. 2. Fantasy.] I. Young, Skottie, illustrator. II. Baum, L. Frank (Lyman Frank), 1856-1919. III. Title.
  PZ7.7.S453Won 2014
  741.5'973--dc23
                                        2013029128

All Spotlight books are reinforced library binding
and manufactured in the United States of America.

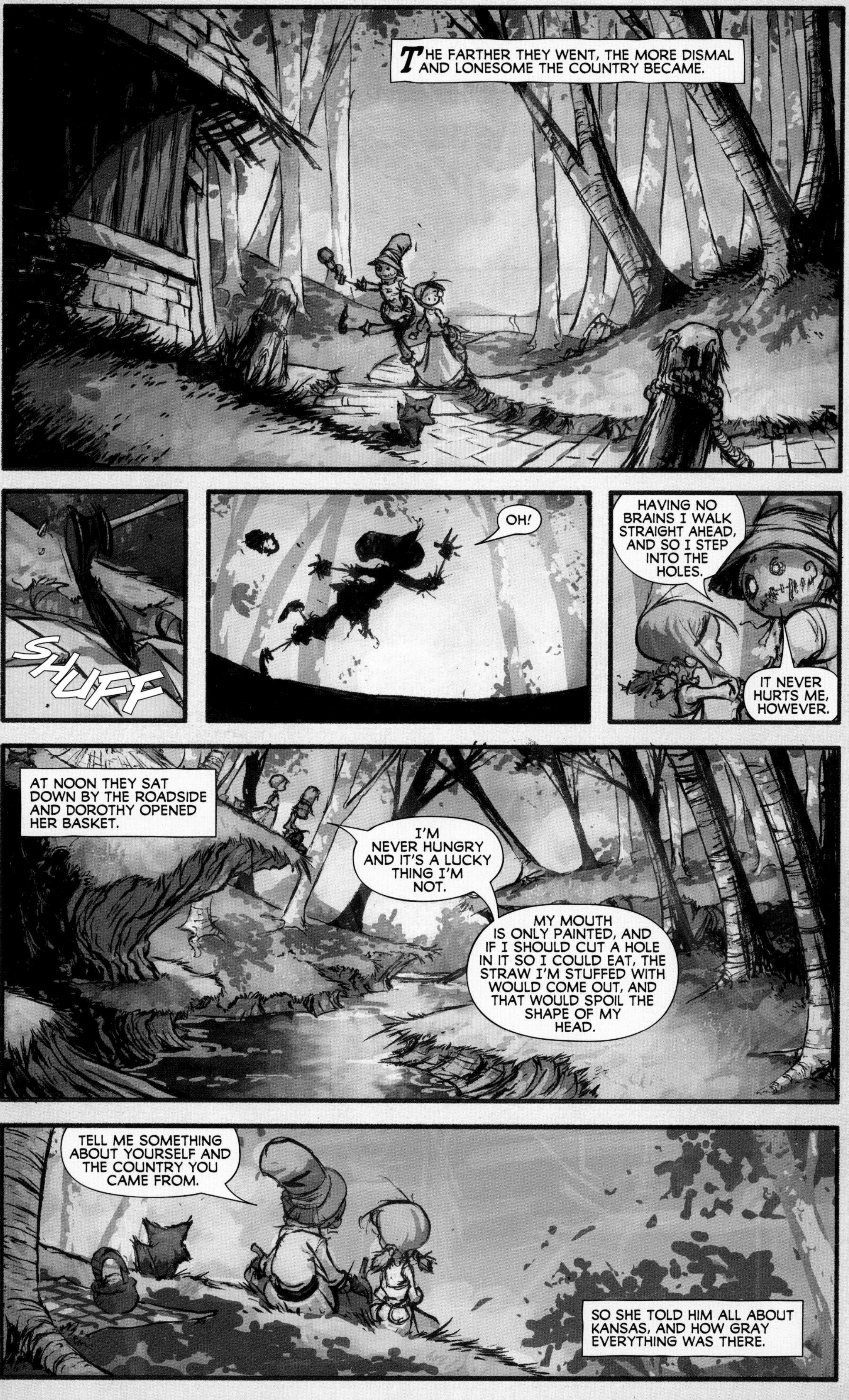
THE FARTHER THEY WENT, THE MORE DISMAL AND LONESOME THE COUNTRY BECAME.
SHUFF
OH!
HAVING NO BRAINS I WALK STRAIGHT AHEAD, AND SO I STEP INTO THE HOLES.
IT NEVER HURTS ME, HOWEVER.
AT NOON THEY SAT DOWN BY THE ROADSIDE AND DOROTHY OPENED HER BASKET.
I'M NEVER HUNGRY AND IT'S A LUCKY THING I'M NOT.
MY MOUTH IS ONLY PAINTED, AND IF I SHOULD CUT A HOLE IN IT SO I COULD EAT, THE STRAW I'M STUFFED WITH WOULD COME OUT, AND THAT WOULD SPOIL THE SHAPE OF MY HEAD.
TELL ME SOMETHING ABOUT YOURSELF AND THE COUNTRY YOU CAME FROM.
SO SHE TOLD HIM ALL ABOUT KANSAS, AND HOW GRAY EVERYTHING WAS THERE.

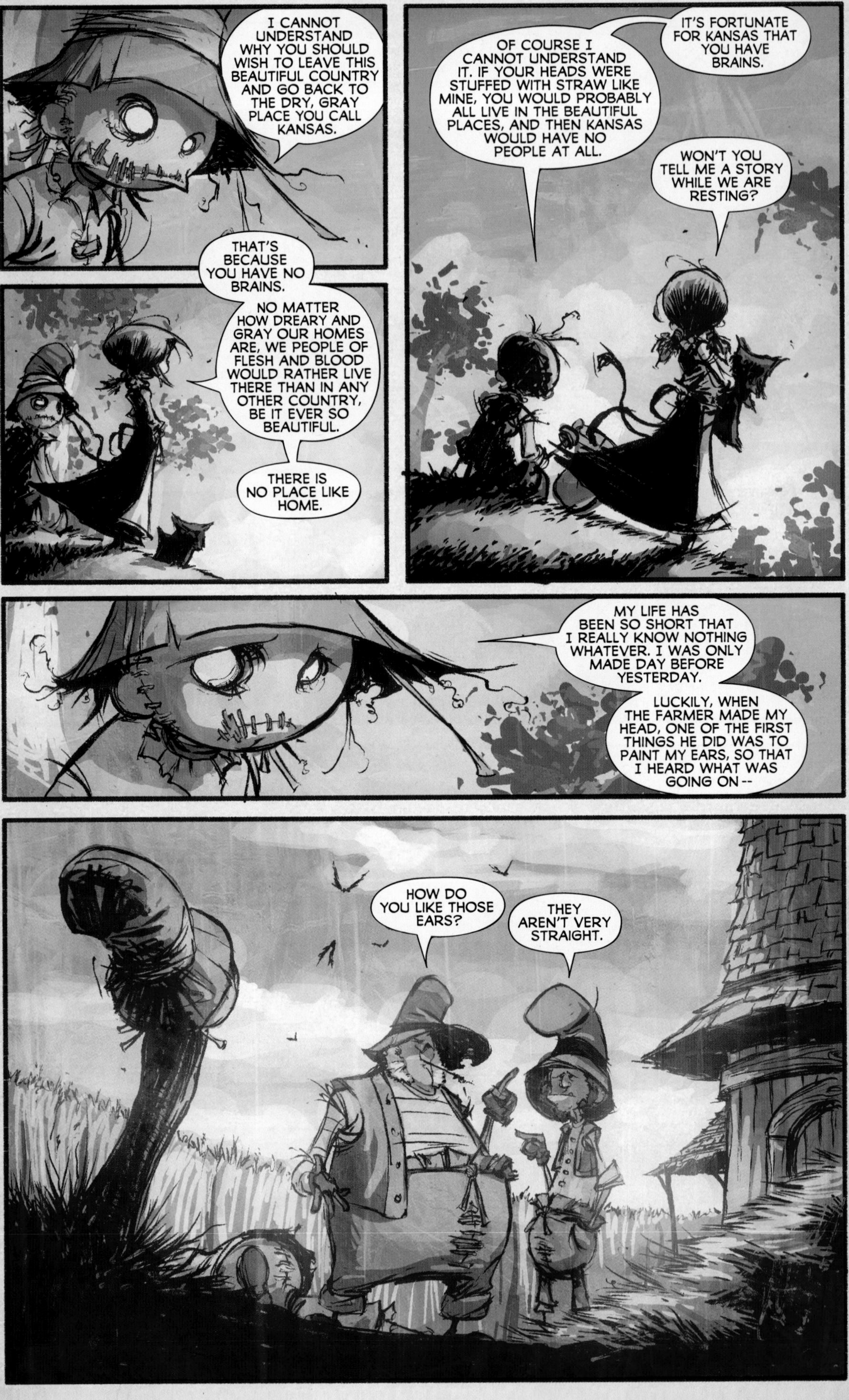
I CANNOT UNDERSTAND WHY YOU SHOULD WISH TO LEAVE THIS BEAUTIFUL COUNTRY AND GO BACK TO THE DRY, GRAY PLACE YOU CALL KANSAS.
THAT'S BECAUSE YOU HAVE NO BRAINS.
NO MATTER HOW DREARY AND GRAY OUR HOMES ARE, WE PEOPLE OF FLESH AND BLOOD WOULD RATHER LIVE THERE THAN IN ANY OTHER COUNTRY, BE IT EVER SO BEAUTIFUL.
THERE IS NO PLACE LIKE HOME.
OF COURSE I CANNOT UNDERSTAND IT. IF YOUR HEADS WERE STUFFED WITH STRAW LIKE MINE, YOU WOULD PROBABLY ALL LIVE IN THE BEAUTIFUL PLACES, AND THEN KANSAS WOULD HAVE NO PEOPLE AT ALL.
IT'S FORTUNATE FOR KANSAS THAT YOU HAVE BRAINS.
WON'T YOU TELL ME A STORY WHILE WE ARE RESTING?
MY LIFE HAS BEEN SO SHORT THAT I REALLY KNOW NOTHING WHATEVER. I WAS ONLY MADE DAY BEFORE YESTERDAY.
LUCKILY, WHEN THE FARMER MADE MY HEAD, ONE OF THE FIRST THINGS HE DID WAS TO PAINT MY EARS, SO THAT I HEARD WHAT WAS GOING ON --
HOW DO YOU LIKE THOSE EARS?
THEY AREN'T VERY STRAIGHT.

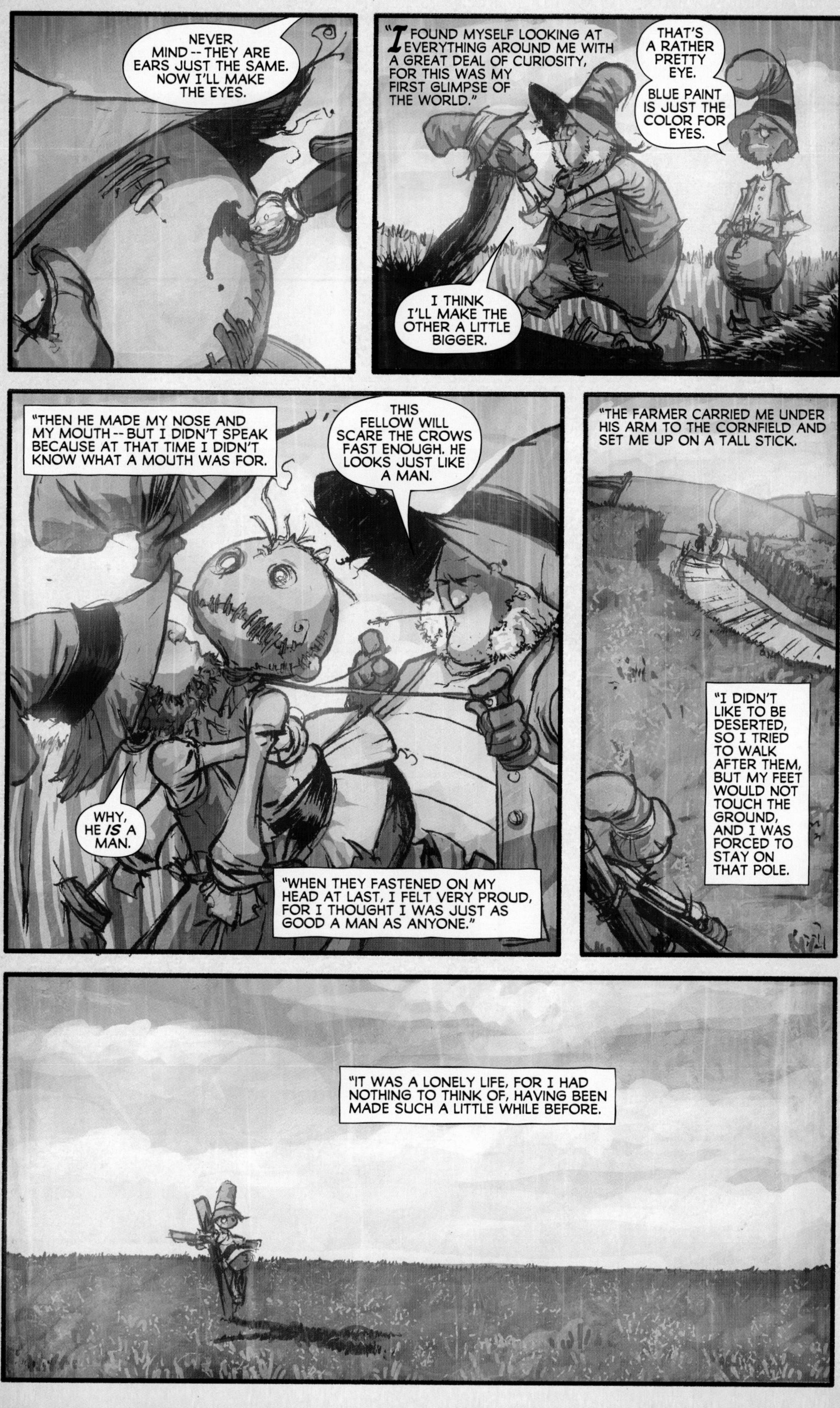
NEVER MIND -- THEY ARE EARS JUST THE SAME. NOW I'LL MAKE THE EYES.
"I FOUND MYSELF LOOKING AT EVERYTHING AROUND ME WITH A GREAT DEAL OF CURIOSITY, FOR THIS WAS MY FIRST GLIMPSE OF THE WORLD."
THAT'S A RATHER PRETTY EYE.
BLUE PAINT IS JUST THE COLOR FOR EYES.
I THINK I'LL MAKE THE OTHER A LITTLE BIGGER.
"THEN HE MADE MY NOSE AND MY MOUTH -- BUT I DIDN'T SPEAK BECAUSE AT THAT TIME I DIDN'T KNOW WHAT A MOUTH WAS FOR.
THIS FELLOW WILL SCARE THE CROWS FAST ENOUGH. HE LOOKS JUST LIKE A MAN.
WHY, HE *IS* A MAN.
"WHEN THEY FASTENED ON MY HEAD AT LAST, I FELT VERY PROUD, FOR I THOUGHT I WAS JUST AS GOOD A MAN AS ANYONE."
"THE FARMER CARRIED ME UNDER HIS ARM TO THE CORNFIELD AND SET ME UP ON A TALL STICK.
"I DIDN'T LIKE TO BE DESERTED, SO I TRIED TO WALK AFTER THEM, BUT MY FEET WOULD NOT TOUCH THE GROUND, AND I WAS FORCED TO STAY ON THAT POLE.
"IT WAS A LONELY LIFE, FOR I HAD NOTHING TO THINK OF, HAVING BEEN MADE SUCH A LITTLE WHILE BEFORE.

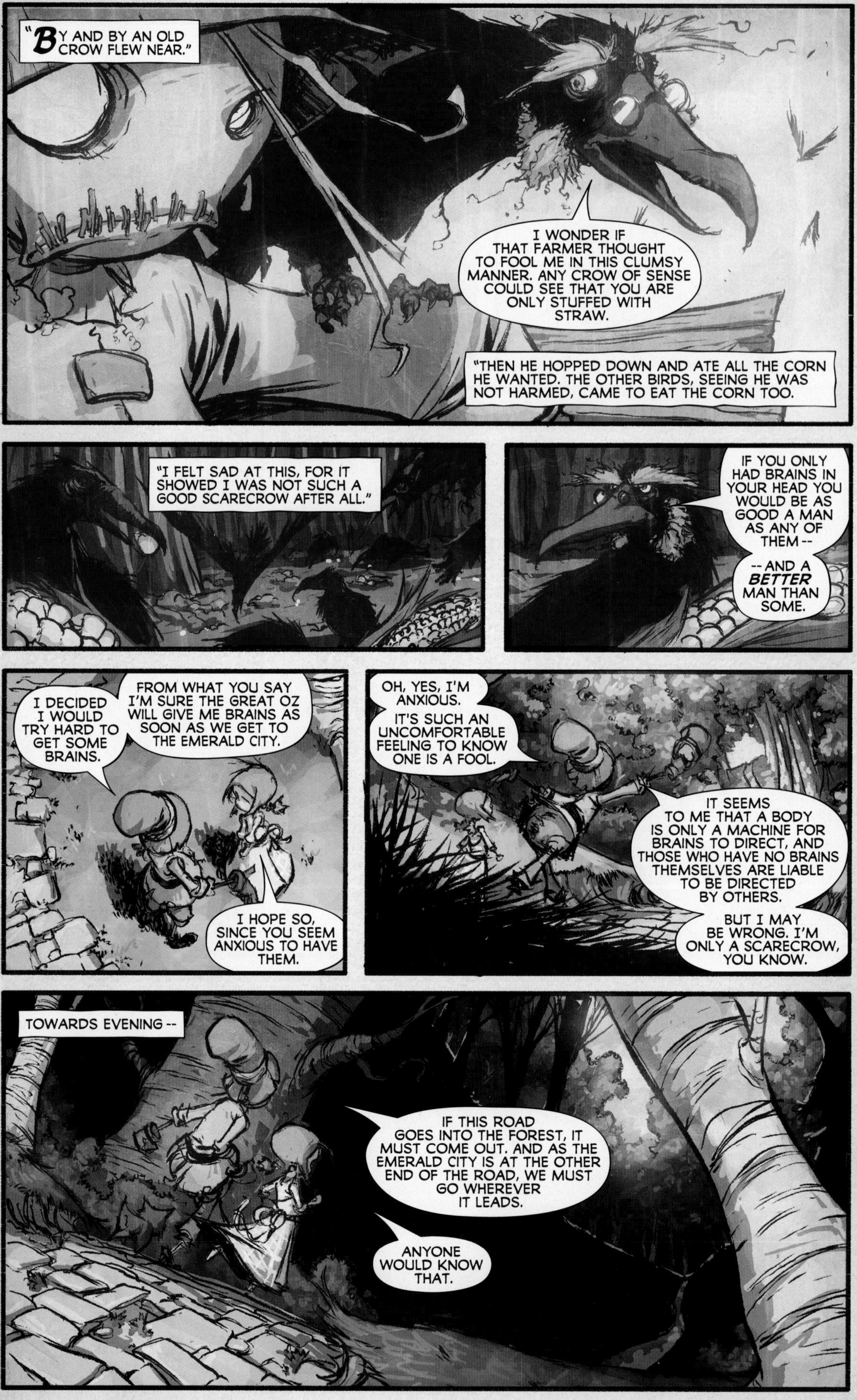
"BY AND BY AN OLD CROW FLEW NEAR."
I WONDER IF THAT FARMER THOUGHT TO FOOL ME IN THIS CLUMSY MANNER. ANY CROW OF SENSE COULD SEE THAT YOU ARE ONLY STUFFED WITH STRAW.
"THEN HE HOPPED DOWN AND ATE ALL THE CORN HE WANTED. THE OTHER BIRDS, SEEING HE WAS NOT HARMED, CAME TO EAT THE CORN TOO.
"I FELT SAD AT THIS, FOR IT SHOWED I WAS NOT SUCH A GOOD SCARECROW AFTER ALL."
IF YOU ONLY HAD BRAINS IN YOUR HEAD YOU WOULD BE AS GOOD A MAN AS ANY OF THEM --
-- AND A *BETTER* MAN THAN SOME.
I DECIDED I WOULD TRY HARD TO GET SOME BRAINS.
FROM WHAT YOU SAY I'M SURE THE GREAT OZ WILL GIVE ME BRAINS AS SOON AS WE GET TO THE EMERALD CITY.
I HOPE SO, SINCE YOU SEEM ANXIOUS TO HAVE THEM.
OH, YES, I'M ANXIOUS.
IT'S SUCH AN UNCOMFORTABLE FEELING TO KNOW ONE IS A FOOL.
IT SEEMS TO ME THAT A BODY IS ONLY A MACHINE FOR BRAINS TO DIRECT, AND THOSE WHO HAVE NO BRAINS THEMSELVES ARE LIABLE TO BE DIRECTED BY OTHERS.
BUT I MAY BE WRONG. I'M ONLY A SCARECROW, YOU KNOW.
TOWARDS EVENING --
IF THIS ROAD GOES INTO THE FOREST, IT MUST COME OUT. AND AS THE EMERALD CITY IS AT THE OTHER END OF THE ROAD, WE MUST GO WHEREVER IT LEADS.
ANYONE WOULD KNOW THAT.

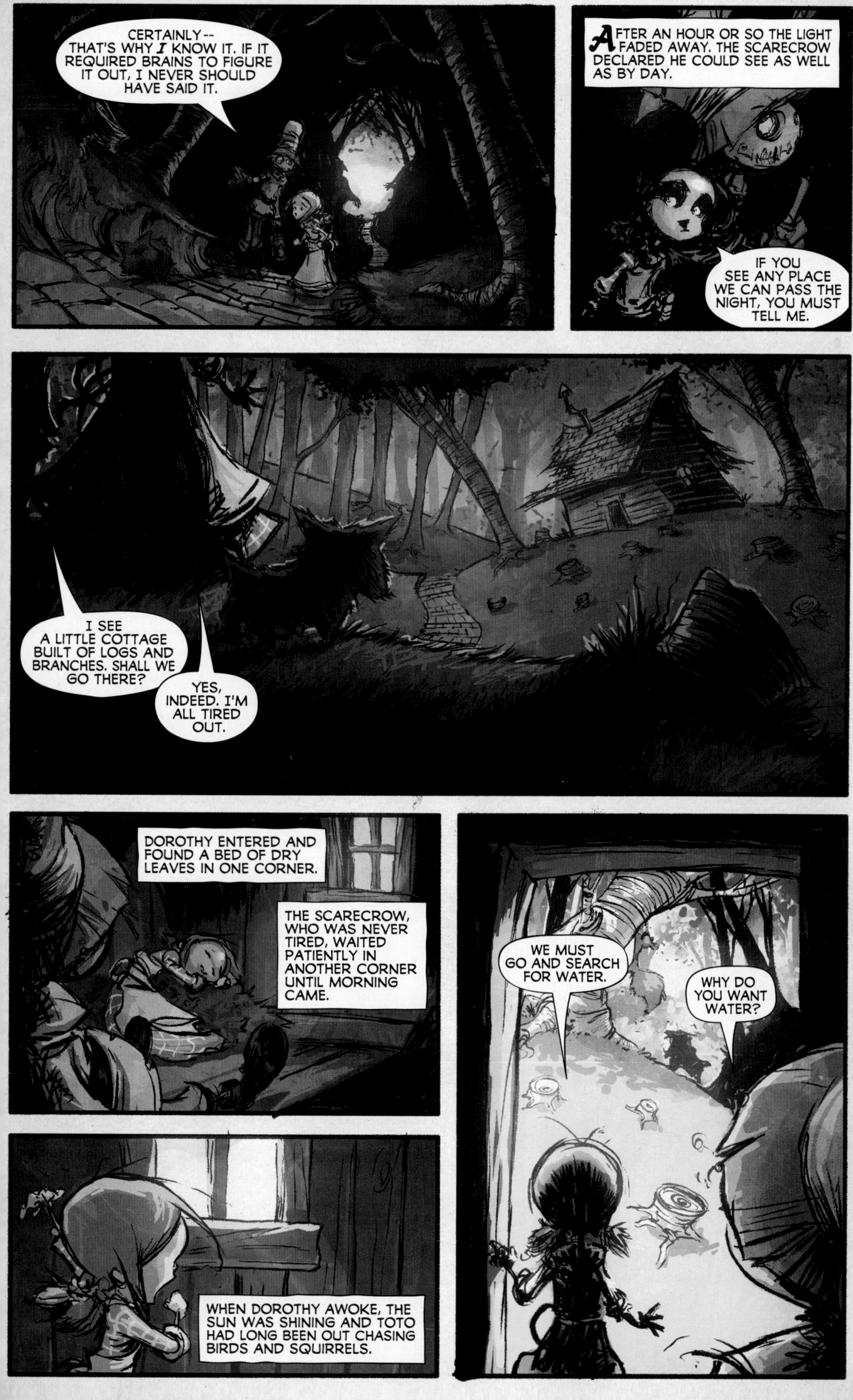
CERTAINLY-- THAT'S WHY I KNOW IT. IF IT REQUIRED BRAINS TO FIGURE IT OUT, I NEVER SHOULD HAVE SAID IT.
AFTER AN HOUR OR SO THE LIGHT FADED AWAY. THE SCARECROW DECLARED HE COULD SEE AS WELL AS BY DAY.
IF YOU SEE ANY PLACE WE CAN PASS THE NIGHT, YOU MUST TELL ME.
I SEE A LITTLE COTTAGE BUILT OF LOGS AND BRANCHES. SHALL WE GO THERE?
YES, INDEED. I'M ALL TIRED OUT.
DOROTHY ENTERED AND FOUND A BED OF DRY LEAVES IN ONE CORNER.
THE SCARECROW, WHO WAS NEVER TIRED, WAITED PATIENTLY IN ANOTHER CORNER UNTIL MORNING CAME.
WHEN DOROTHY AWOKE, THE SUN WAS SHINING AND TOTO HAD LONG BEEN OUT CHASING BIRDS AND SQUIRRELS.
WE MUST GO AND SEARCH FOR WATER.
WHY DO YOU WANT WATER?

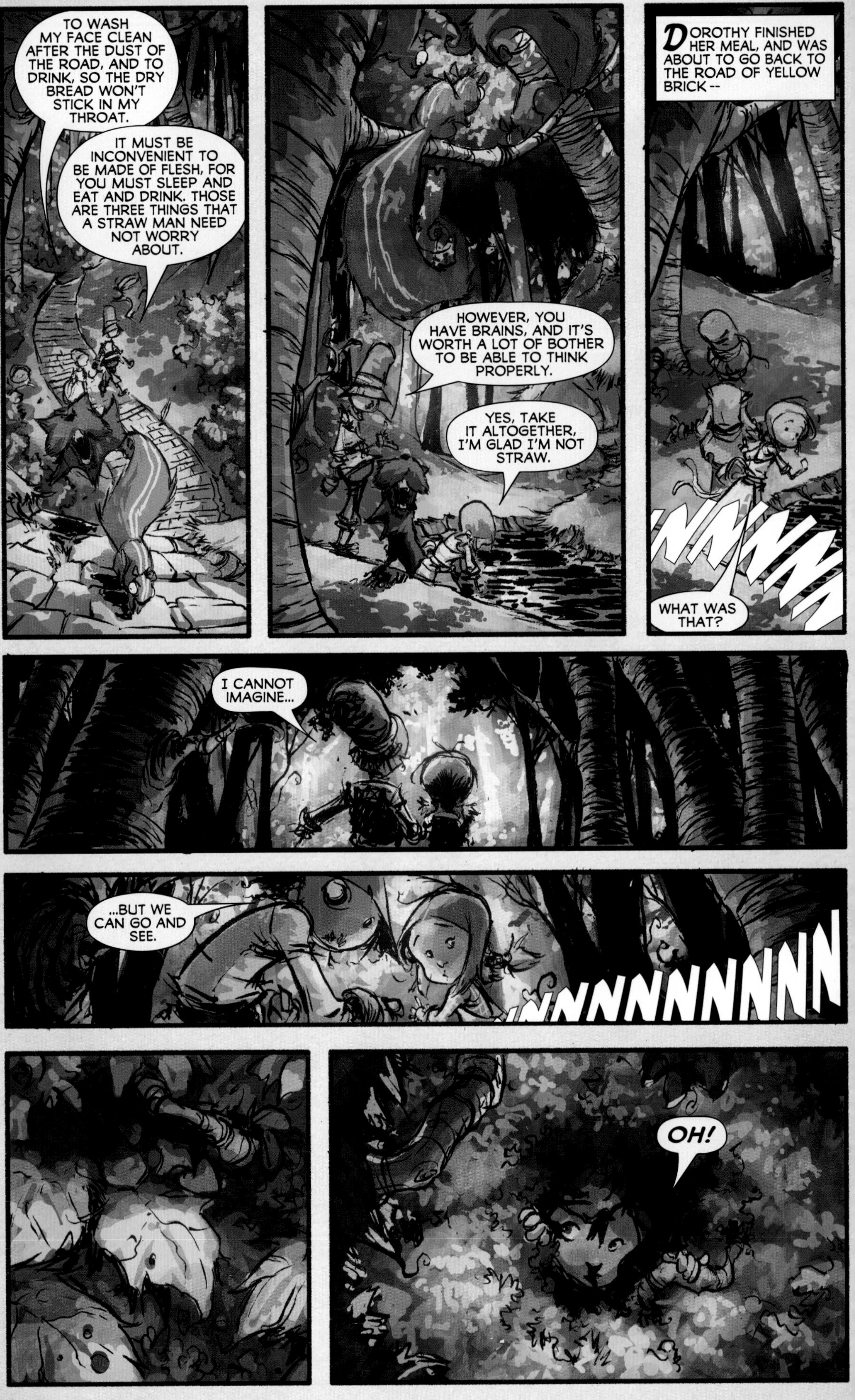
TO WASH MY FACE CLEAN AFTER THE DUST OF THE ROAD, AND TO DRINK, SO THE DRY BREAD WON'T STICK IN MY THROAT.
IT MUST BE INCONVENIENT TO BE MADE OF FLESH, FOR YOU MUST SLEEP AND EAT AND DRINK. THOSE ARE THREE THINGS THAT A STRAW MAN NEED NOT WORRY ABOUT.
HOWEVER, YOU HAVE BRAINS, AND IT'S WORTH A LOT OF BOTHER TO BE ABLE TO THINK PROPERLY.
YES, TAKE IT ALTOGETHER, I'M GLAD I'M NOT STRAW.
DOROTHY FINISHED HER MEAL, AND WAS ABOUT TO GO BACK TO THE ROAD OF YELLOW BRICK --
NNNNNN
WHAT WAS THAT?
I CANNOT IMAGINE...
...BUT WE CAN GO AND SEE.
NNNNNNNNNNN
OH!

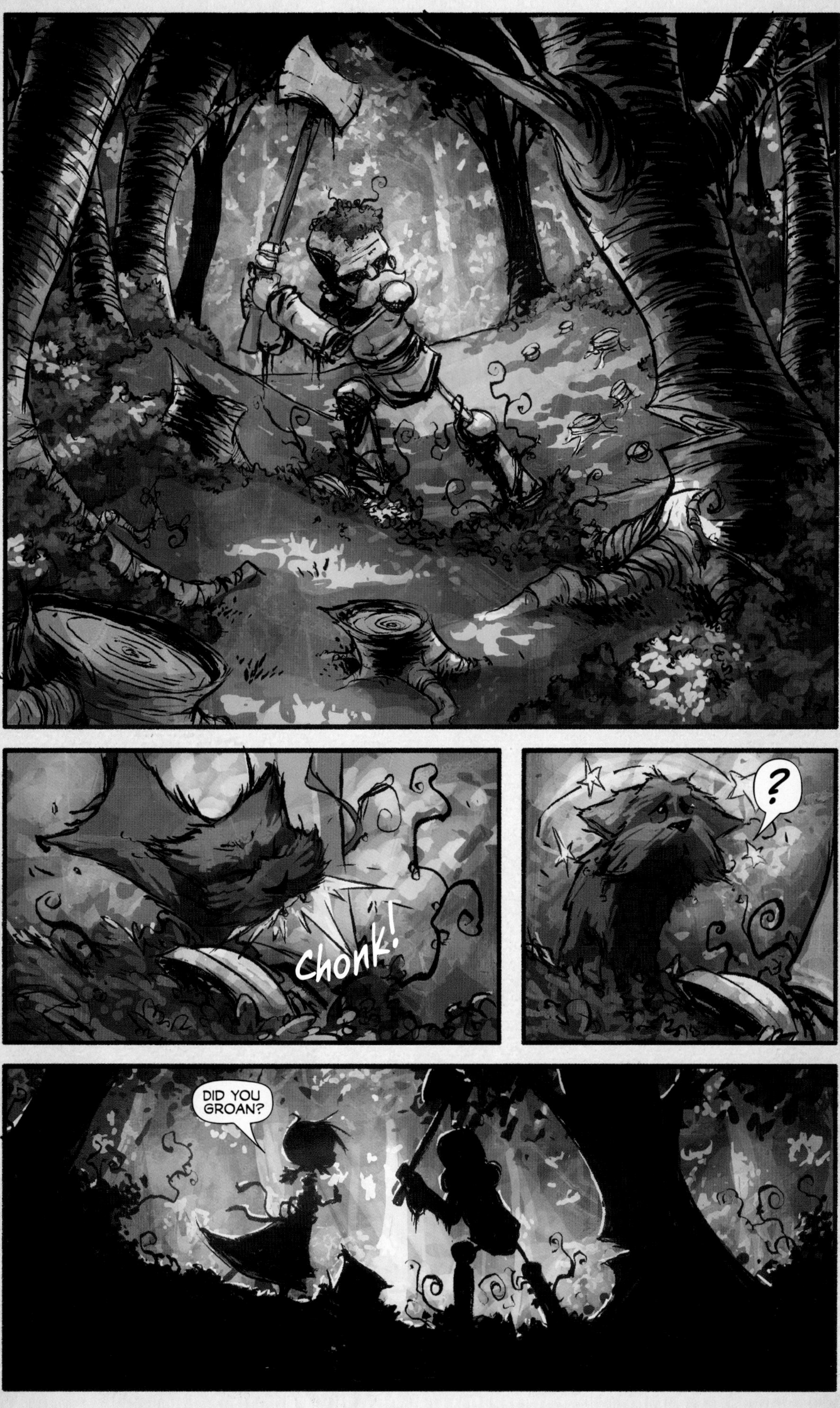
Chonk!
?
DID YOU GROAN?

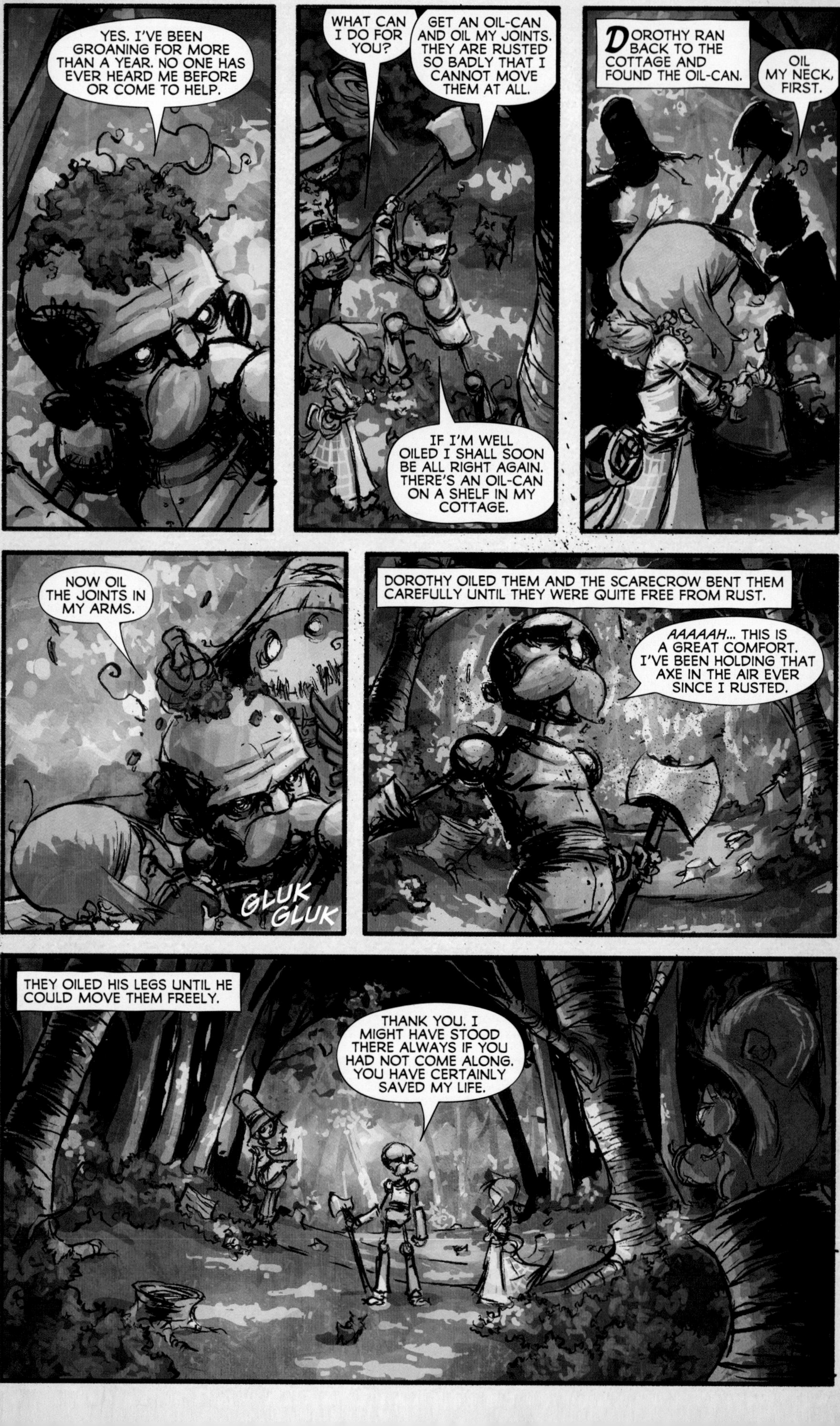
YES. I'VE BEEN GROANING FOR MORE THAN A YEAR. NO ONE HAS EVER HEARD ME BEFORE OR COME TO HELP.
WHAT CAN I DO FOR YOU?
GET AN OIL-CAN AND OIL MY JOINTS. THEY ARE RUSTED SO BADLY THAT I CANNOT MOVE THEM AT ALL.
IF I'M WELL OILED I SHALL SOON BE ALL RIGHT AGAIN. THERE'S AN OIL-CAN ON A SHELF IN MY COTTAGE.
DOROTHY RAN BACK TO THE COTTAGE AND FOUND THE OIL-CAN.
OIL MY NECK, FIRST.
NOW OIL THE JOINTS IN MY ARMS.
GLUK GLUK
DOROTHY OILED THEM AND THE SCARECROW BENT THEM CAREFULLY UNTIL THEY WERE QUITE FREE FROM RUST.
AAAAAH... THIS IS A GREAT COMFORT. I'VE BEEN HOLDING THAT AXE IN THE AIR EVER SINCE I RUSTED.
THEY OILED HIS LEGS UNTIL HE COULD MOVE THEM FREELY.
THANK YOU. I MIGHT HAVE STOOD THERE ALWAYS IF YOU HAD NOT COME ALONG. YOU HAVE CERTAINLY SAVED MY LIFE.

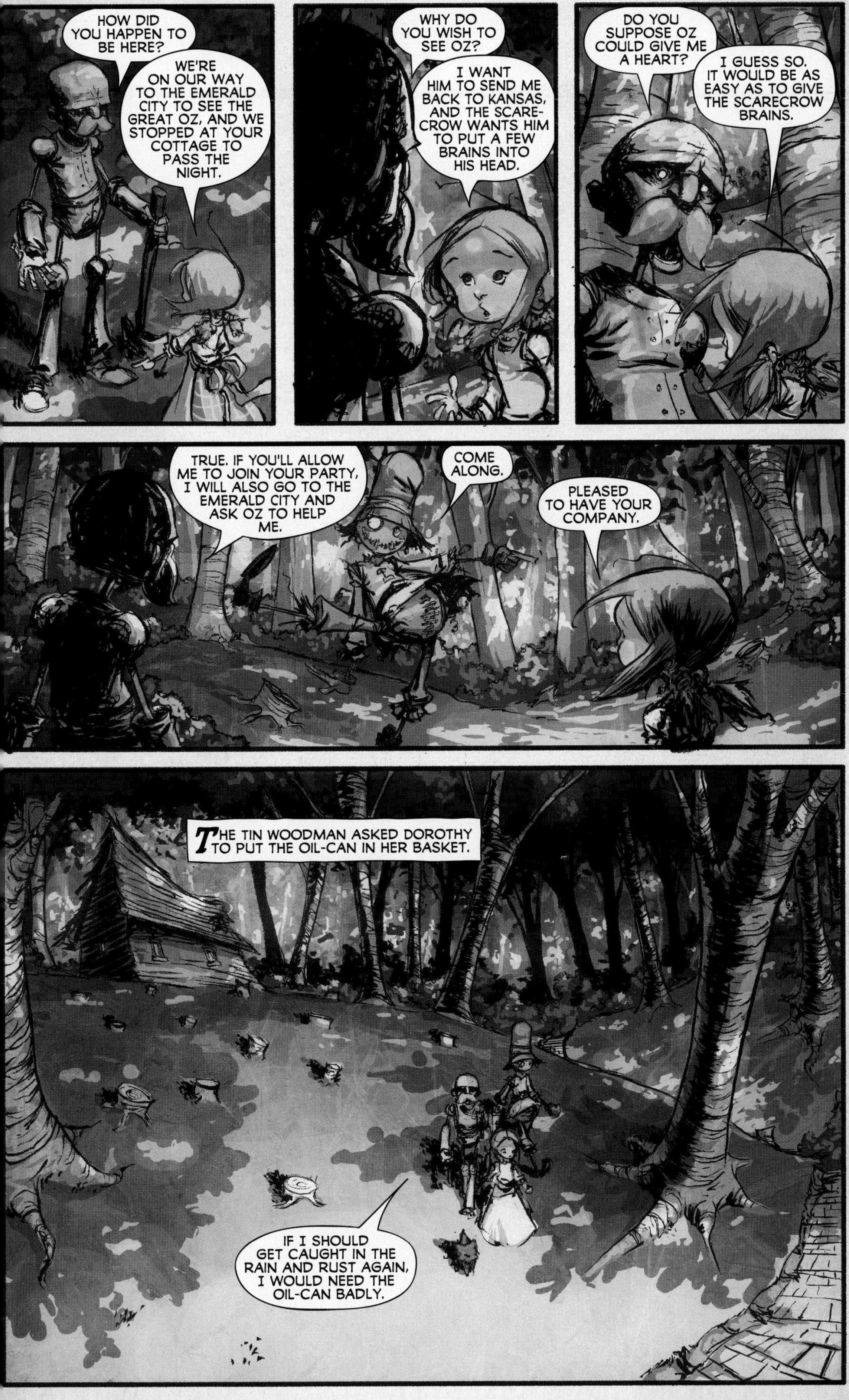
HOW DID YOU HAPPEN TO BE HERE?
WE'RE ON OUR WAY TO THE EMERALD CITY TO SEE THE GREAT OZ, AND WE STOPPED AT YOUR COTTAGE TO PASS THE NIGHT.
WHY DO YOU WISH TO SEE OZ?
I WANT HIM TO SEND ME BACK TO KANSAS, AND THE SCARE-CROW WANTS HIM TO PUT A FEW BRAINS INTO HIS HEAD.
DO YOU SUPPOSE OZ COULD GIVE ME A HEART?
I GUESS SO. IT WOULD BE AS EASY AS TO GIVE THE SCARECROW BRAINS.
TRUE. IF YOU'LL ALLOW ME TO JOIN YOUR PARTY, I WILL ALSO GO TO THE EMERALD CITY AND ASK OZ TO HELP ME.
COME ALONG.
PLEASED TO HAVE YOUR COMPANY.
THE TIN WOODMAN ASKED DOROTHY TO PUT THE OIL-CAN IN HER BASKET.
IF I SHOULD GET CAUGHT IN THE RAIN AND RUST AGAIN, I WOULD NEED THE OIL-CAN BADLY.

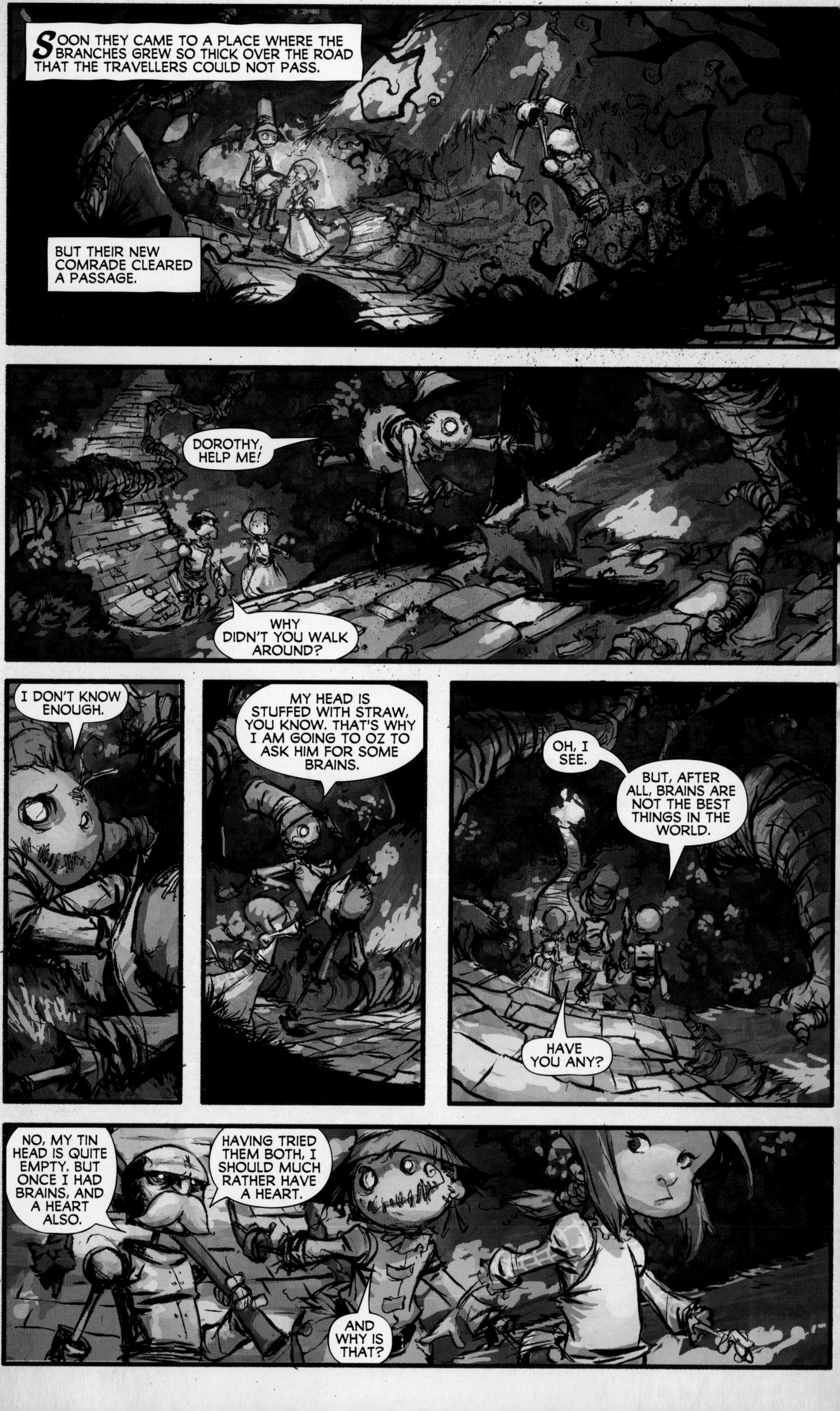
SOON THEY CAME TO A PLACE WHERE THE BRANCHES GREW SO THICK OVER THE ROAD THAT THE TRAVELLERS COULD NOT PASS.
BUT THEIR NEW COMRADE CLEARED A PASSAGE.
DOROTHY, HELP ME!
WHY DIDN'T YOU WALK AROUND?
I DON'T KNOW ENOUGH.
MY HEAD IS STUFFED WITH STRAW, YOU KNOW. THAT'S WHY I AM GOING TO OZ TO ASK HIM FOR SOME BRAINS.
OH, I SEE.
BUT, AFTER ALL, BRAINS ARE NOT THE BEST THINGS IN THE WORLD.
HAVE YOU ANY?
NO, MY TIN HEAD IS QUITE EMPTY. BUT ONCE I HAD BRAINS, AND A HEART ALSO.
HAVING TRIED THEM BOTH, I SHOULD MUCH RATHER HAVE A HEART.
AND WHY IS THAT?

I'LL TELL YOU MY STORY, AND THEN YOU WILL KNOW.

I WAS BORN THE SON OF A WOODMAN WHO CHOPPED DOWN TREES AND SOLD THE WOOD FOR A LIVING. WHEN I GREW UP I TOO BECAME A WOOD-CHOPPER.

AFTER MY PARENTS DIED, I MADE UP MY MIND THAT I WOULD MARRY, SO THAT I MIGHT NOT BECOME LONELY.

"ONE OF THE MUNCHKIN GIRLS WAS SO BEAUTIFUL THAT I SOON GREW TO LOVE HER WITH ALL MY HEART.

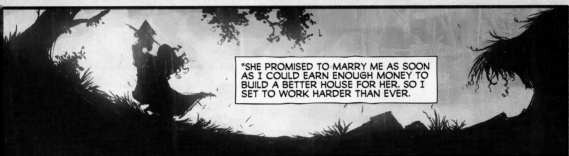

"SHE PROMISED TO MARRY ME AS SOON AS I COULD EARN ENOUGH MONEY TO BUILD A BETTER HOUSE FOR HER. SO I SET TO WORK HARDER THAN EVER.

"BUT THE GIRL LIVED WITH AN OLD WOMAN WHO DIDN'T WANT HER TO MARRY, FOR SHE WAS SO LAZY SHE WISHED THE GIRL TO REMAIN AND DO THE COOKING AND HOUSEWORK.

"THE OLD WOMAN WENT TO THE WICKED WITCH OF THE EAST AND PROMISED HER TWO SHEEP AND A COW IF SHE WOULD PREVENT THE MARRIAGE. THEREUPON, THE WITCH ENCHANTED MY AXE.

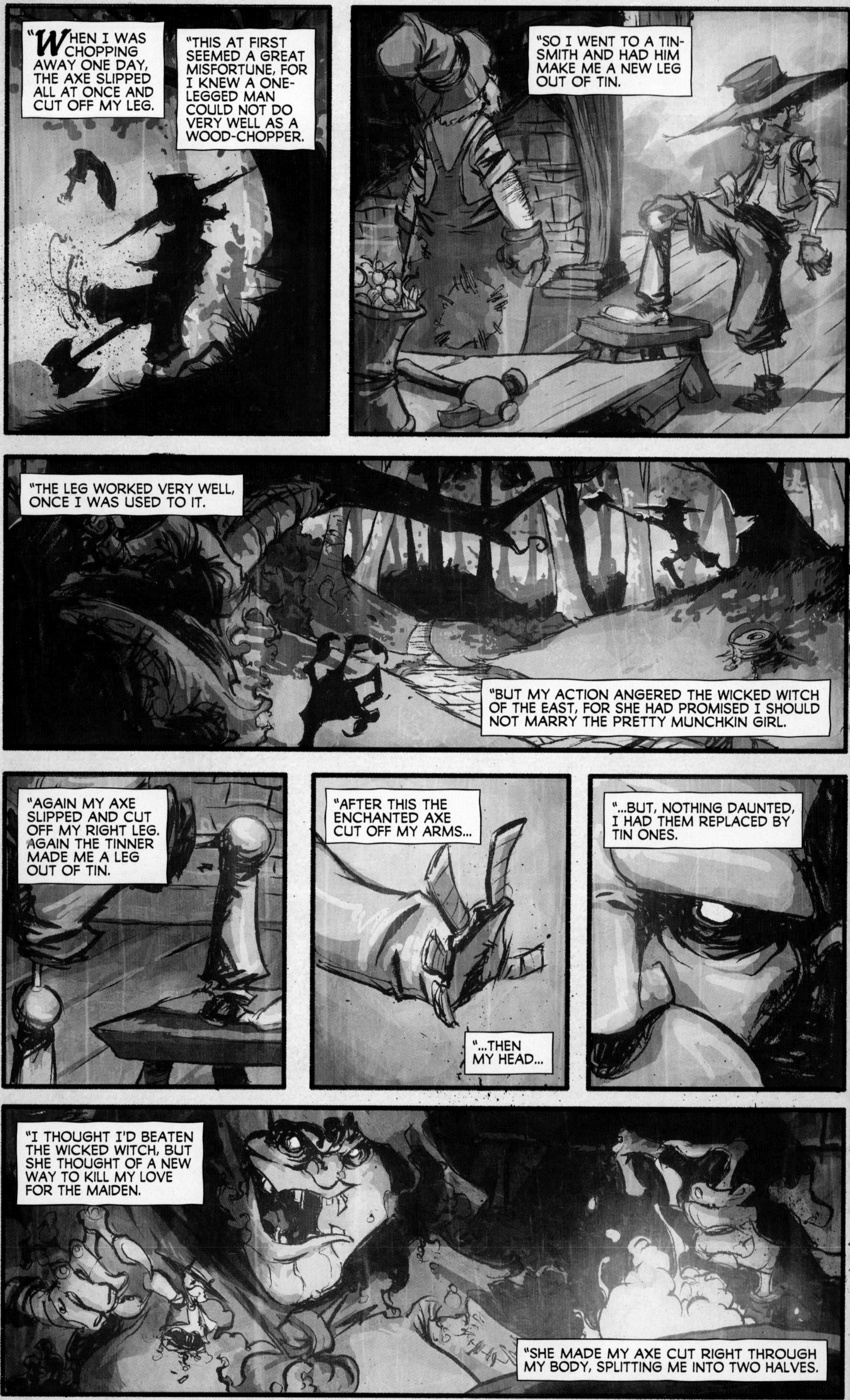
"When I was chopping away one day, the axe slipped all at once and cut off my leg.
"This at first seemed a great misfortune, for I knew a one-legged man could not do very well as a wood-chopper.
"So I went to a tin-smith and had him make me a new leg out of tin.
"The leg worked very well, once I was used to it.
"But my action angered the Wicked Witch of the East, for she had promised I should not marry the pretty Munchkin girl.
"Again my axe slipped and cut off my right leg. Again the tinner made me a leg out of tin.
"After this the enchanted axe cut off my arms...
"...then my head...
"...But, nothing daunted, I had them replaced by tin ones.
"I thought I'd beaten the Wicked Witch, but she thought of a new way to kill my love for the maiden.
"She made my axe cut right through my body, splitting me into two halves.

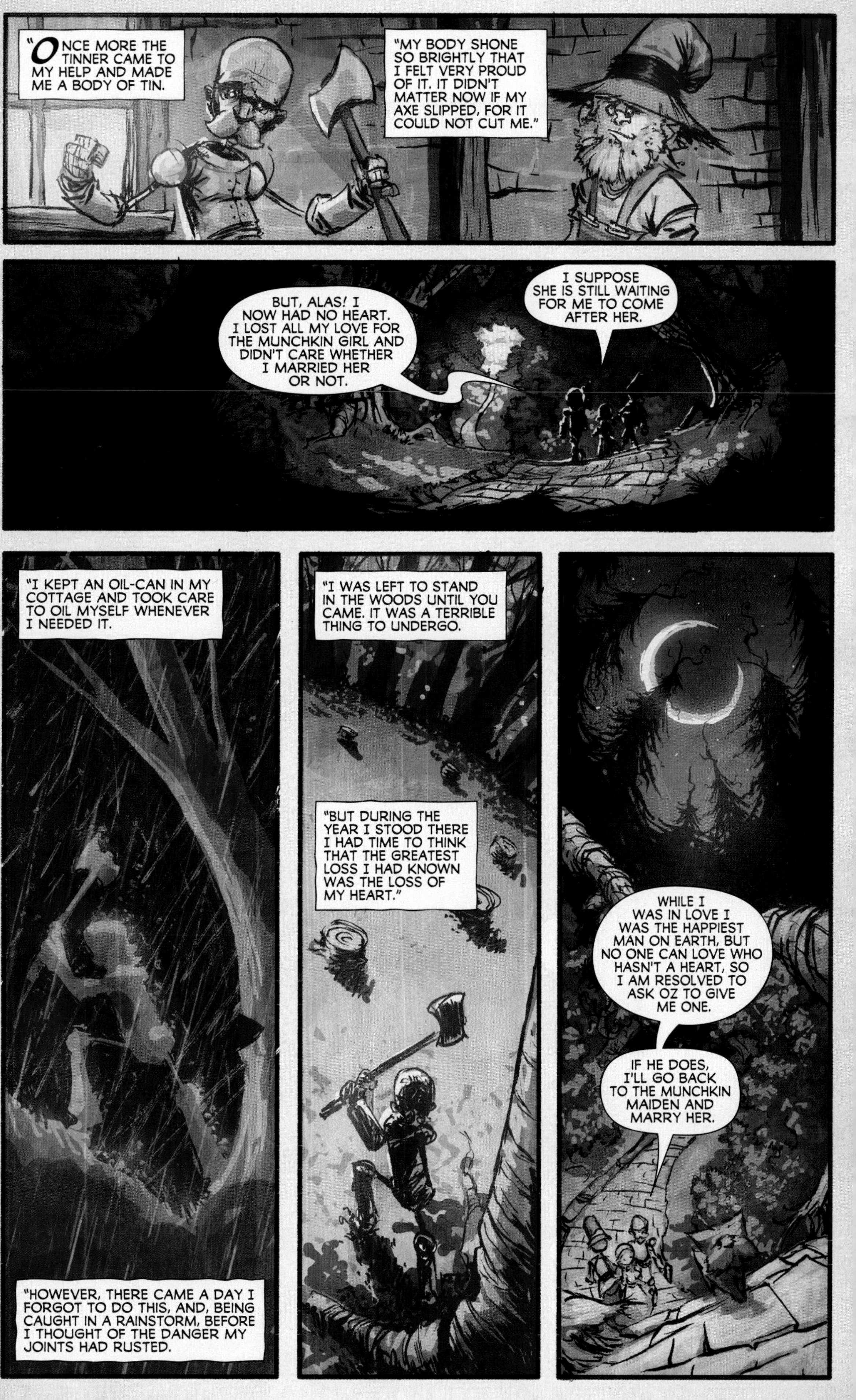
"ONCE MORE THE TINNER CAME TO MY HELP AND MADE ME A BODY OF TIN.
"MY BODY SHONE SO BRIGHTLY THAT I FELT VERY PROUD OF IT. IT DIDN'T MATTER NOW IF MY AXE SLIPPED, FOR IT COULD NOT CUT ME."
BUT, ALAS! I NOW HAD NO HEART. I LOST ALL MY LOVE FOR THE MUNCHKIN GIRL AND DIDN'T CARE WHETHER I MARRIED HER OR NOT.
I SUPPOSE SHE IS STILL WAITING FOR ME TO COME AFTER HER.
"I KEPT AN OIL-CAN IN MY COTTAGE AND TOOK CARE TO OIL MYSELF WHENEVER I NEEDED IT.
"HOWEVER, THERE CAME A DAY I FORGOT TO DO THIS, AND, BEING CAUGHT IN A RAINSTORM, BEFORE I THOUGHT OF THE DANGER MY JOINTS HAD RUSTED.
"I WAS LEFT TO STAND IN THE WOODS UNTIL YOU CAME. IT WAS A TERRIBLE THING TO UNDERGO.
"BUT DURING THE YEAR I STOOD THERE I HAD TIME TO THINK THAT THE GREATEST LOSS I HAD KNOWN WAS THE LOSS OF MY HEART."
WHILE I WAS IN LOVE I WAS THE HAPPIEST MAN ON EARTH, BUT NO ONE CAN LOVE WHO HASN'T A HEART, SO I AM RESOLVED TO ASK OZ TO GIVE ME ONE.
IF HE DOES, I'LL GO BACK TO THE MUNCHKIN MAIDEN AND MARRY HER.

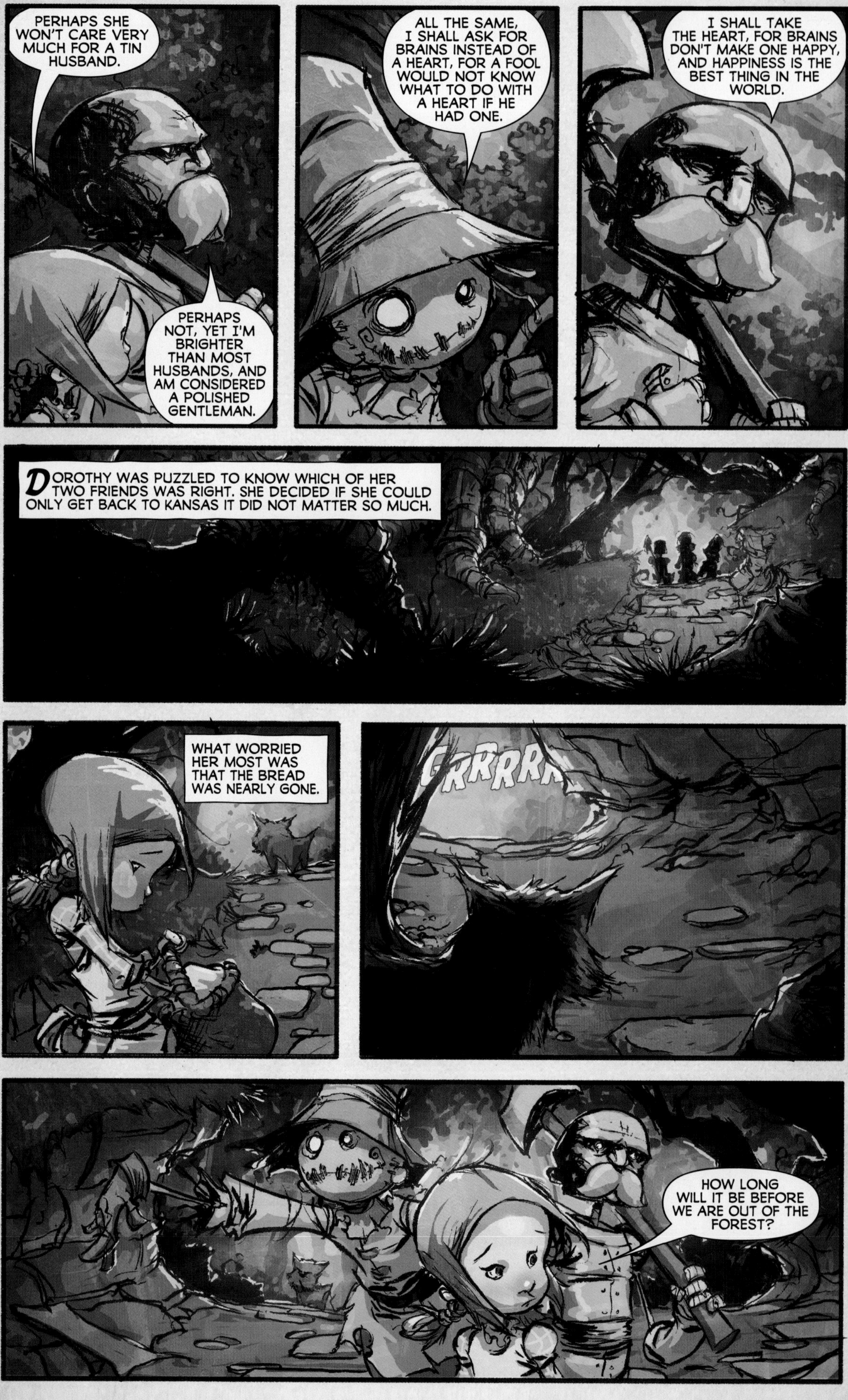
PERHAPS SHE WON'T CARE VERY MUCH FOR A TIN HUSBAND.
PERHAPS NOT, YET I'M BRIGHTER THAN MOST HUSBANDS, AND AM CONSIDERED A POLISHED GENTLEMAN.
ALL THE SAME, I SHALL ASK FOR BRAINS INSTEAD OF A HEART, FOR A FOOL WOULD NOT KNOW WHAT TO DO WITH A HEART IF HE HAD ONE.
I SHALL TAKE THE HEART, FOR BRAINS DON'T MAKE ONE HAPPY, AND HAPPINESS IS THE BEST THING IN THE WORLD.
DOROTHY WAS PUZZLED TO KNOW WHICH OF HER TWO FRIENDS WAS RIGHT. SHE DECIDED IF SHE COULD ONLY GET BACK TO KANSAS IT DID NOT MATTER SO MUCH.
WHAT WORRIED HER MOST WAS THAT THE BREAD WAS NEARLY GONE.
GRRRRR
HOW LONG WILL IT BE BEFORE WE ARE OUT OF THE FOREST?

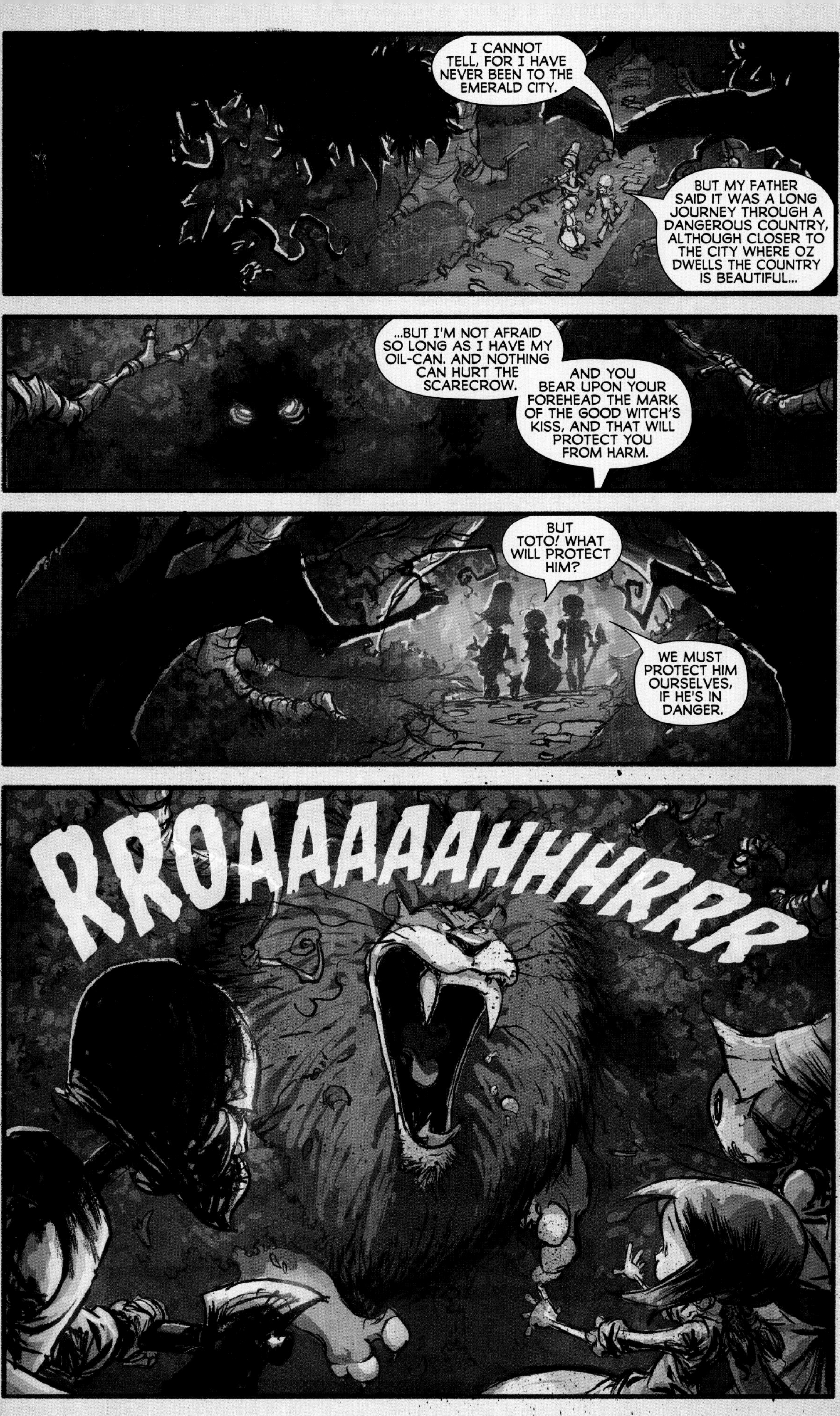
I CANNOT TELL, FOR I HAVE NEVER BEEN TO THE EMERALD CITY.
BUT MY FATHER SAID IT WAS A LONG JOURNEY THROUGH A DANGEROUS COUNTRY, ALTHOUGH CLOSER TO THE CITY WHERE OZ DWELLS THE COUNTRY IS BEAUTIFUL...
...BUT I'M NOT AFRAID SO LONG AS I HAVE MY OIL-CAN. AND NOTHING CAN HURT THE SCARECROW.
AND YOU BEAR UPON YOUR FOREHEAD THE MARK OF THE GOOD WITCH'S KISS, AND THAT WILL PROTECT YOU FROM HARM.
BUT TOTO! WHAT WILL PROTECT HIM?
WE MUST PROTECT HIM OURSELVES, IF HE'S IN DANGER.
RROAAAAAAHHHRRR

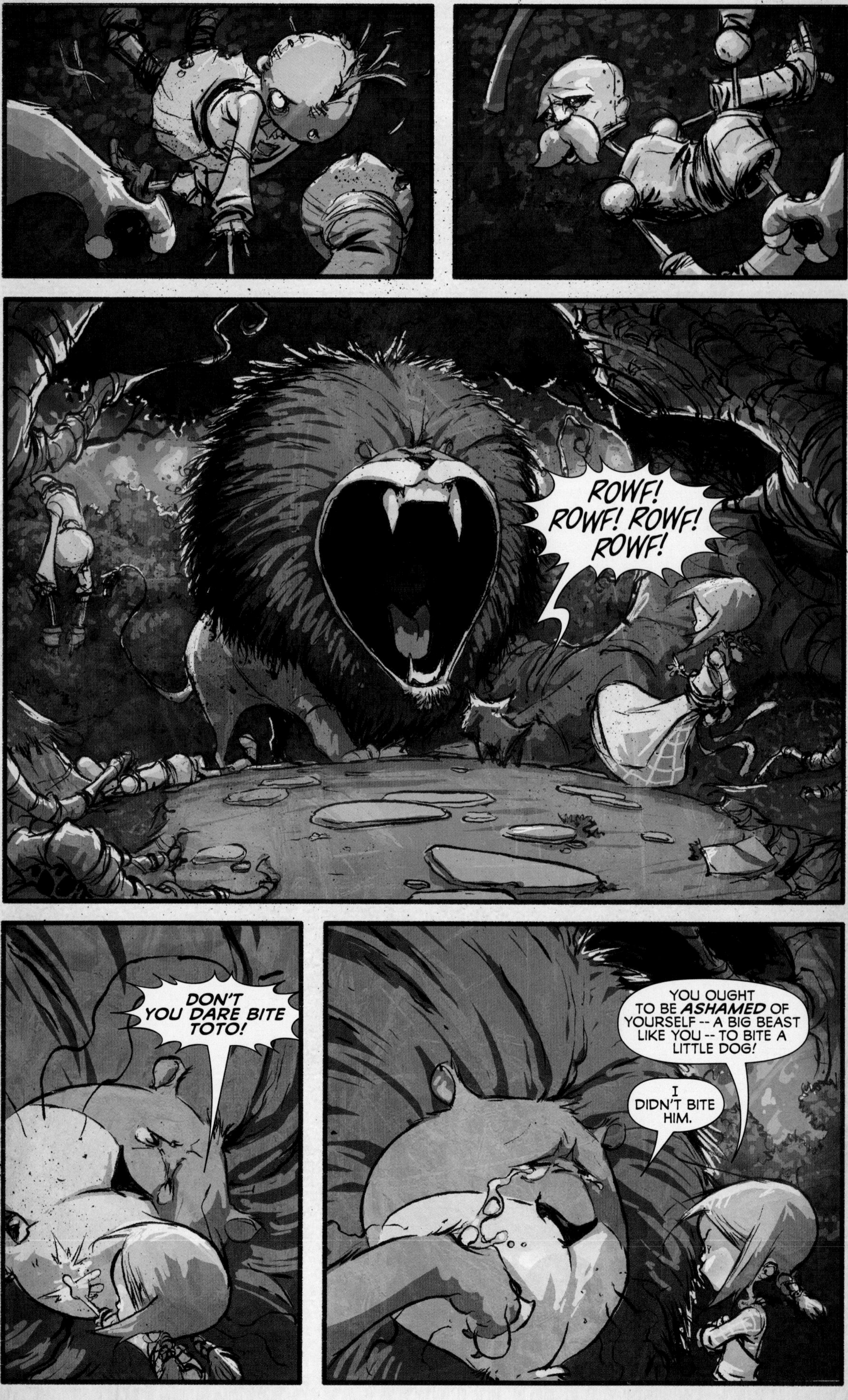
ROWF! ROWF! ROWF! ROWF!
DON'T YOU DARE BITE TOTO!
YOU OUGHT TO BE **ASHAMED** OF YOURSELF -- A BIG BEAST LIKE YOU -- TO BITE A LITTLE DOG!
I DIDN'T BITE HIM.

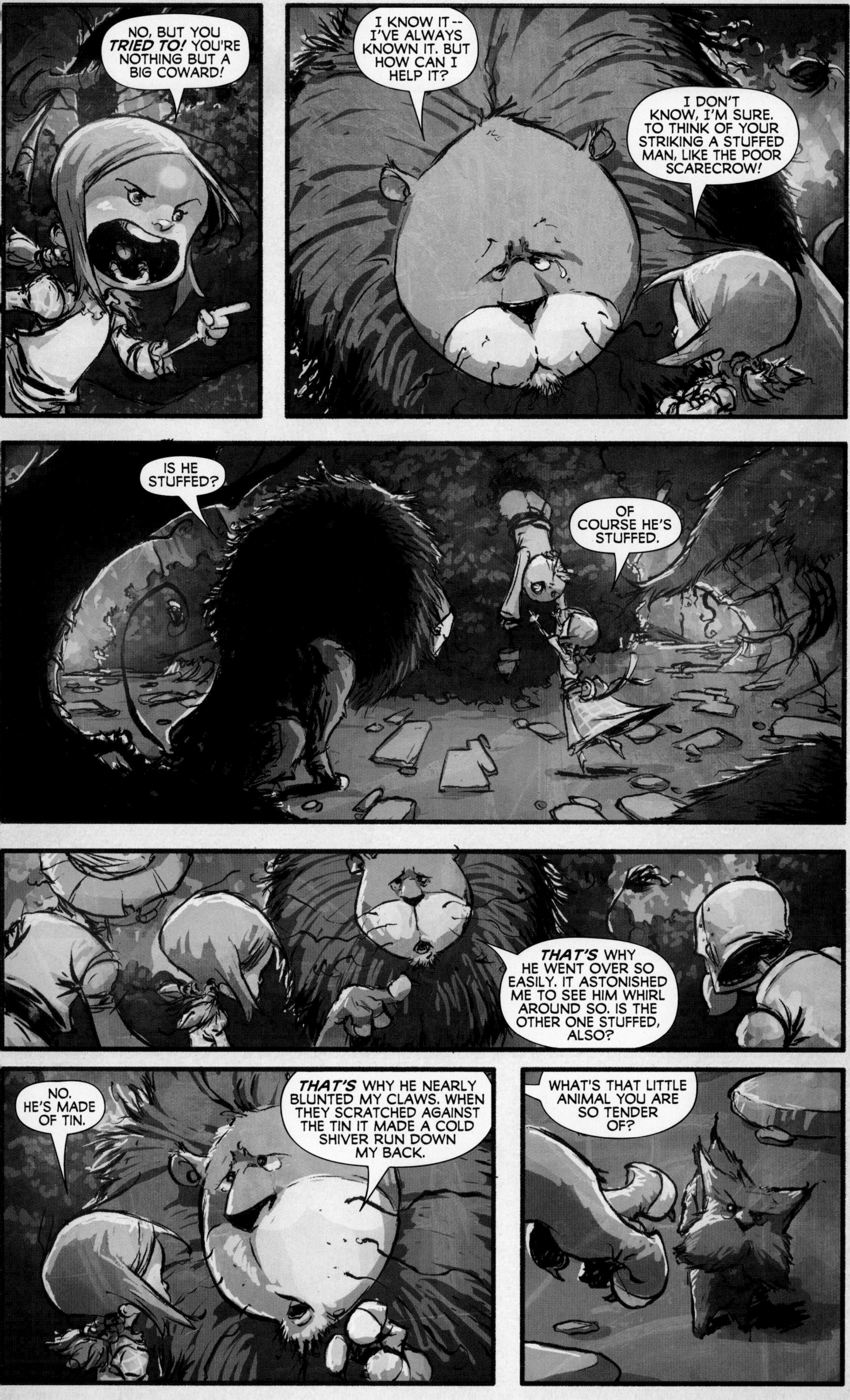
NO, BUT YOU *TRIED TO!* YOU'RE NOTHING BUT A BIG COWARD!
I KNOW IT -- I'VE ALWAYS KNOWN IT. BUT HOW CAN I HELP IT?
I DON'T KNOW, I'M SURE. TO THINK OF YOUR STRIKING A STUFFED MAN, LIKE THE POOR SCARECROW!
IS HE STUFFED?
OF COURSE HE'S STUFFED.
THAT'S WHY HE WENT OVER SO EASILY. IT ASTONISHED ME TO SEE HIM WHIRL AROUND SO. IS THE OTHER ONE STUFFED, ALSO?
NO. HE'S MADE OF TIN.
THAT'S WHY HE NEARLY BLUNTED MY CLAWS. WHEN THEY SCRATCHED AGAINST THE TIN IT MADE A COLD SHIVER RUN DOWN MY BACK.
WHAT'S THAT LITTLE ANIMAL YOU ARE SO TENDER OF?

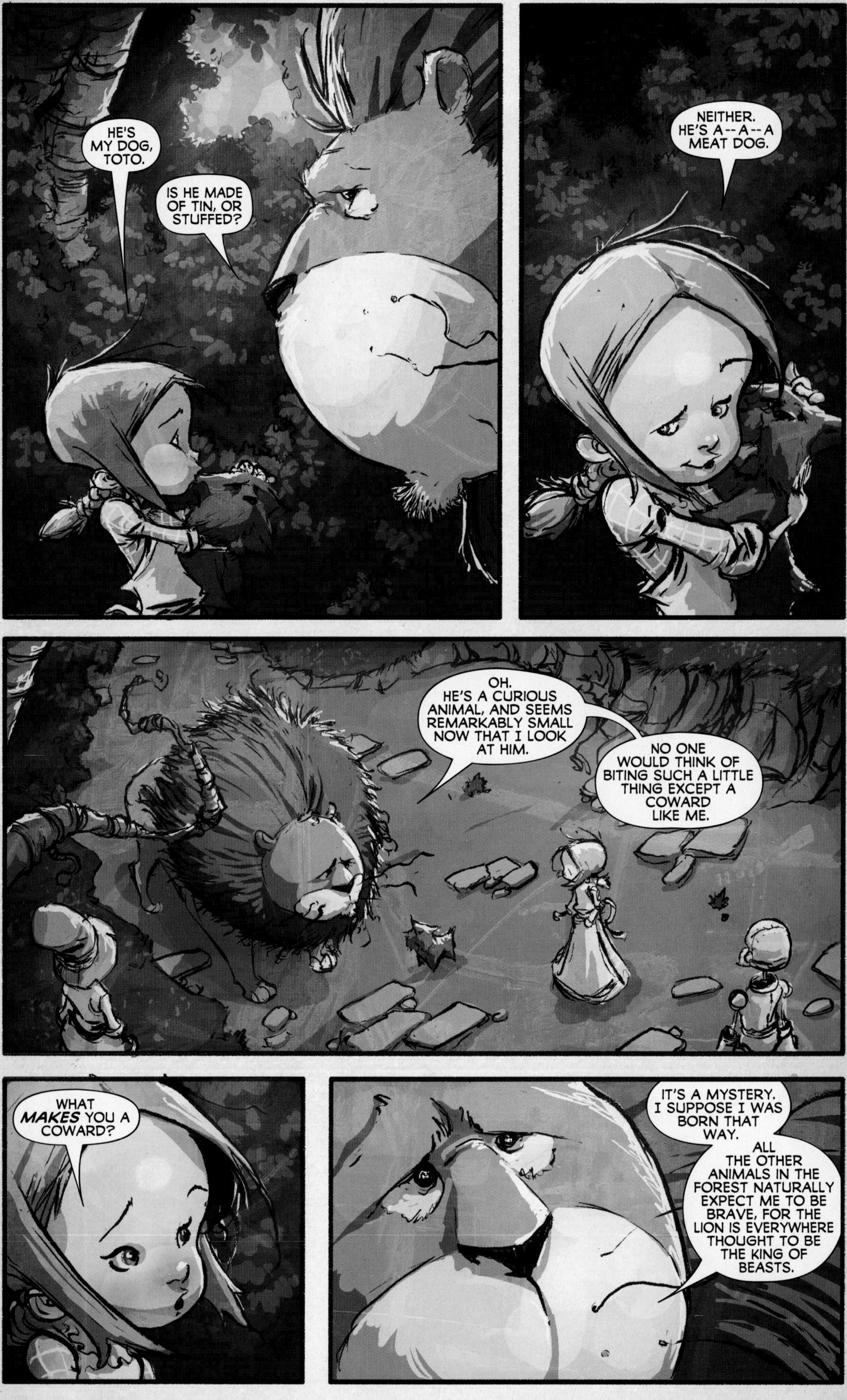
HE'S MY DOG, TOTO.
IS HE MADE OF TIN, OR STUFFED?
NEITHER. HE'S A--A--A MEAT DOG.
OH. HE'S A CURIOUS ANIMAL, AND SEEMS REMARKABLY SMALL NOW THAT I LOOK AT HIM.
NO ONE WOULD THINK OF BITING SUCH A LITTLE THING EXCEPT A COWARD LIKE ME.
WHAT *MAKES* YOU A COWARD?
IT'S A MYSTERY. I SUPPOSE I WAS BORN THAT WAY.
ALL THE OTHER ANIMALS IN THE FOREST NATURALLY EXPECT ME TO BE BRAVE, FOR THE LION IS EVERYWHERE THOUGHT TO BE THE KING OF BEASTS.

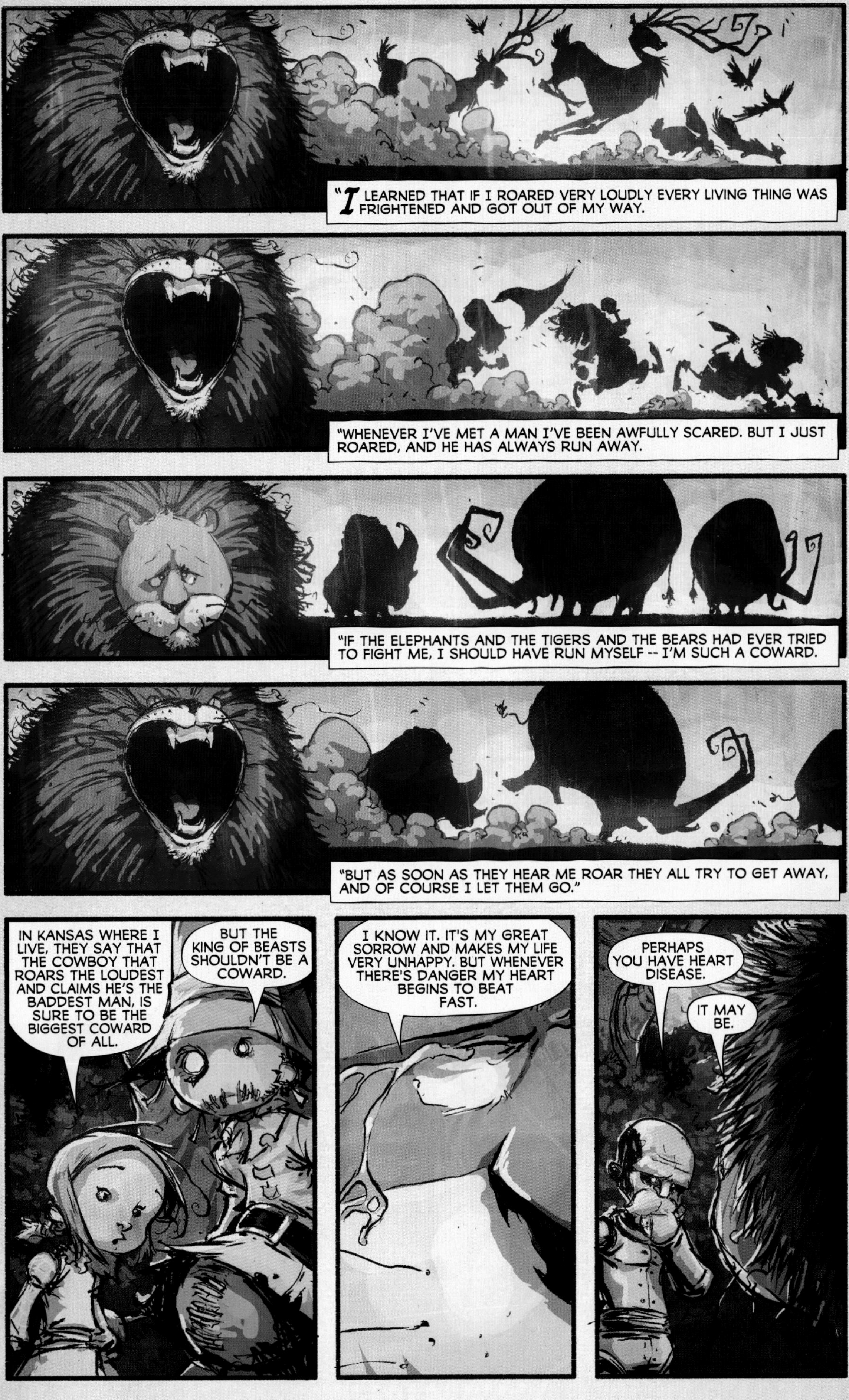
"I LEARNED THAT IF I ROARED VERY LOUDLY EVERY LIVING THING WAS FRIGHTENED AND GOT OUT OF MY WAY.
"WHENEVER I'VE MET A MAN I'VE BEEN AWFULLY SCARED. BUT I JUST ROARED, AND HE HAS ALWAYS RUN AWAY.
"IF THE ELEPHANTS AND THE TIGERS AND THE BEARS HAD EVER TRIED TO FIGHT ME, I SHOULD HAVE RUN MYSELF -- I'M SUCH A COWARD.
"BUT AS SOON AS THEY HEAR ME ROAR THEY ALL TRY TO GET AWAY, AND OF COURSE I LET THEM GO."
IN KANSAS WHERE I LIVE, THEY SAY THAT THE COWBOY THAT ROARS THE LOUDEST AND CLAIMS HE'S THE BADDEST MAN, IS SURE TO BE THE BIGGEST COWARD OF ALL.
BUT THE KING OF BEASTS SHOULDN'T BE A COWARD.
I KNOW IT. IT'S MY GREAT SORROW AND MAKES MY LIFE VERY UNHAPPY. BUT WHENEVER THERE'S DANGER MY HEART BEGINS TO BEAT FAST.
PERHAPS YOU HAVE HEART DISEASE.
IT MAY BE.

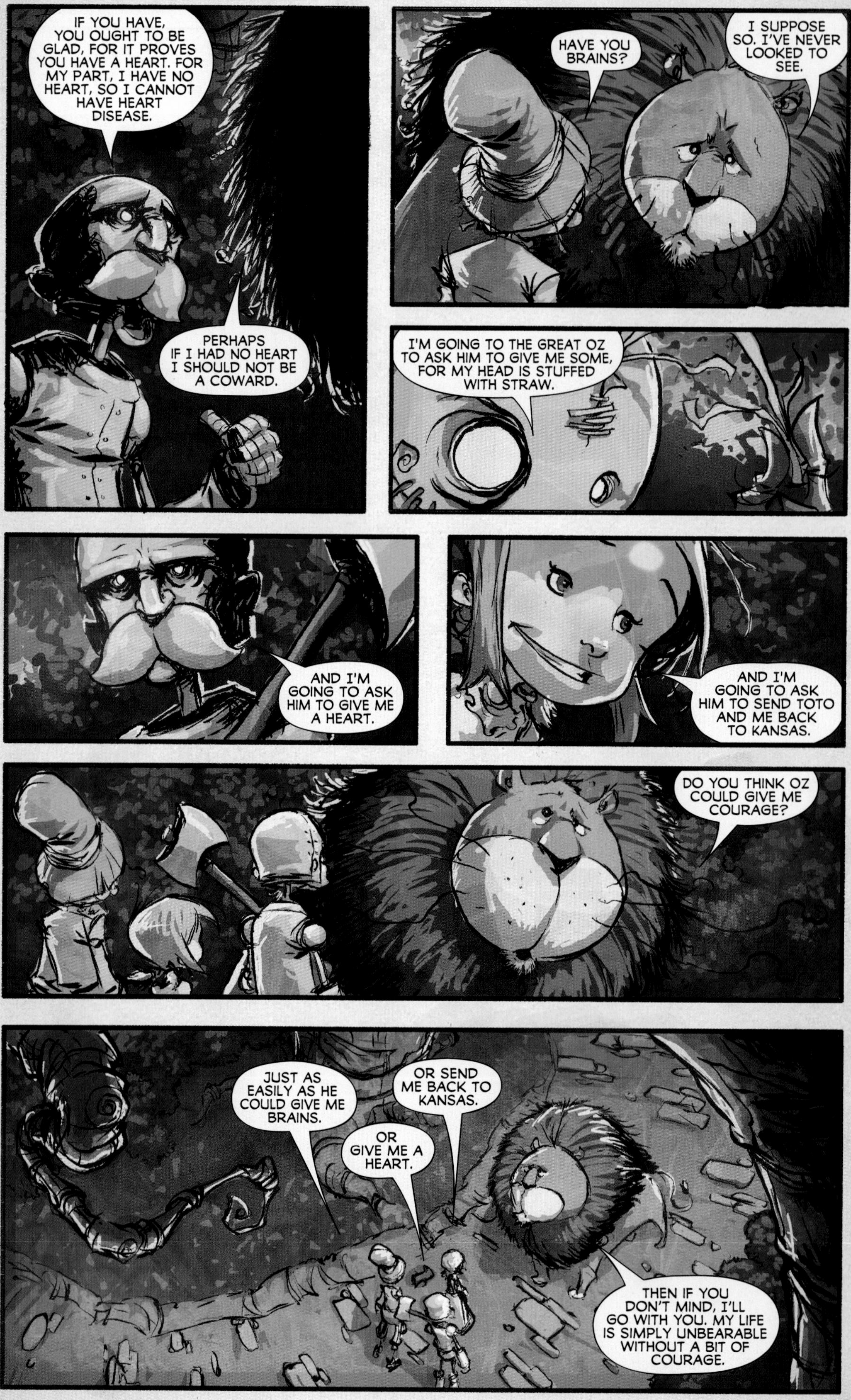
IF YOU HAVE, YOU OUGHT TO BE GLAD, FOR IT PROVES YOU HAVE A HEART. FOR MY PART, I HAVE NO HEART, SO I CANNOT HAVE HEART DISEASE.
PERHAPS IF I HAD NO HEART I SHOULD NOT BE A COWARD.
HAVE YOU BRAINS?
I SUPPOSE SO. I'VE NEVER LOOKED TO SEE.
I'M GOING TO THE GREAT OZ TO ASK HIM TO GIVE ME SOME, FOR MY HEAD IS STUFFED WITH STRAW.
AND I'M GOING TO ASK HIM TO GIVE ME A HEART.
AND I'M GOING TO ASK HIM TO SEND TOTO AND ME BACK TO KANSAS.
DO YOU THINK OZ COULD GIVE ME COURAGE?
JUST AS EASILY AS HE COULD GIVE ME BRAINS.
OR GIVE ME A HEART.
OR SEND ME BACK TO KANSAS.
THEN IF YOU DON'T MIND, I'LL GO WITH YOU. MY LIFE IS SIMPLY UNBEARABLE WITHOUT A BIT OF COURAGE.

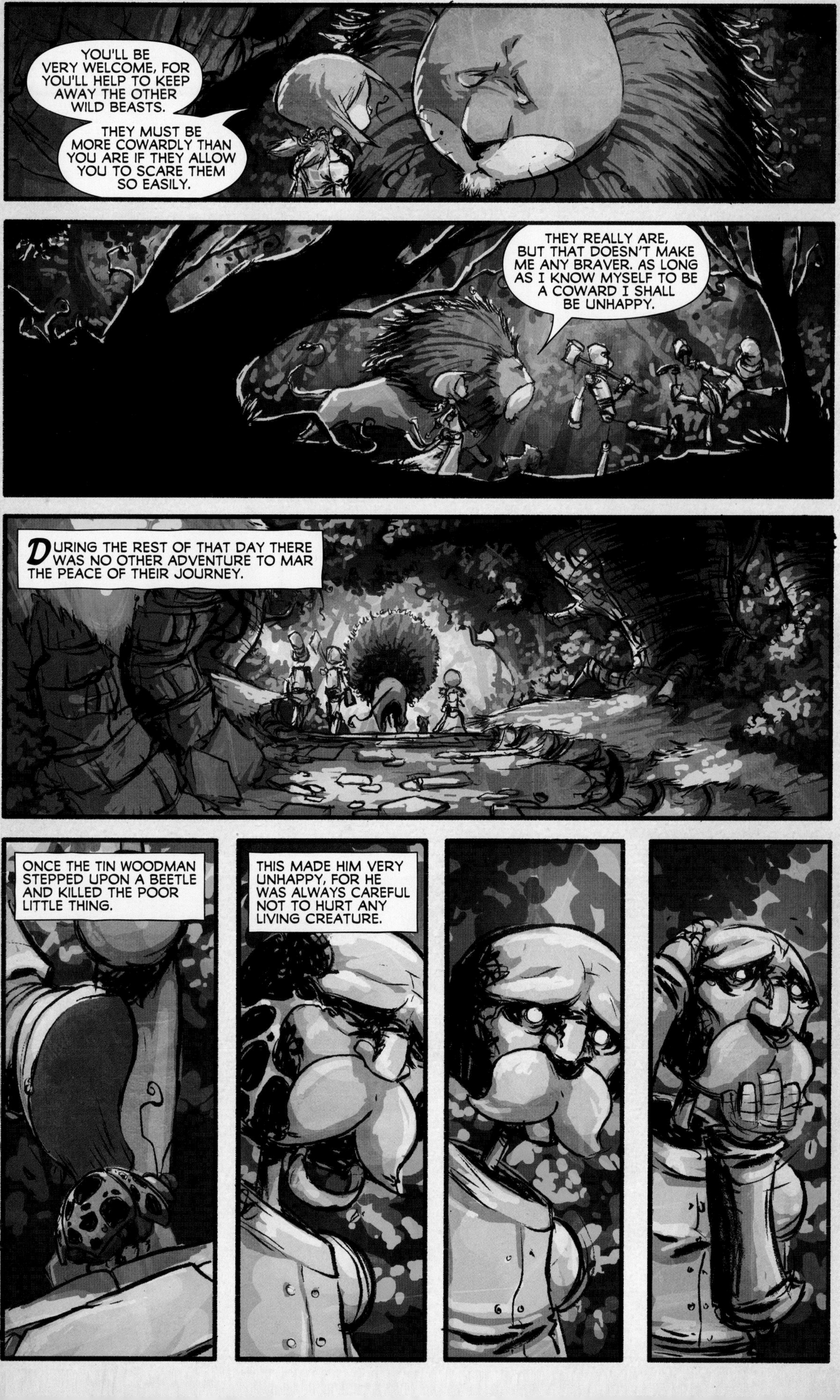
YOU'LL BE VERY WELCOME, FOR YOU'LL HELP TO KEEP AWAY THE OTHER WILD BEASTS.
THEY MUST BE MORE COWARDLY THAN YOU ARE IF THEY ALLOW YOU TO SCARE THEM SO EASILY.
THEY REALLY ARE, BUT THAT DOESN'T MAKE ME ANY BRAVER. AS LONG AS I KNOW MYSELF TO BE A COWARD I SHALL BE UNHAPPY.
DURING THE REST OF THAT DAY THERE WAS NO OTHER ADVENTURE TO MAR THE PEACE OF THEIR JOURNEY.
ONCE THE TIN WOODMAN STEPPED UPON A BEETLE AND KILLED THE POOR LITTLE THING.
THIS MADE HIM VERY UNHAPPY, FOR HE WAS ALWAYS CAREFUL NOT TO HURT ANY LIVING CREATURE.

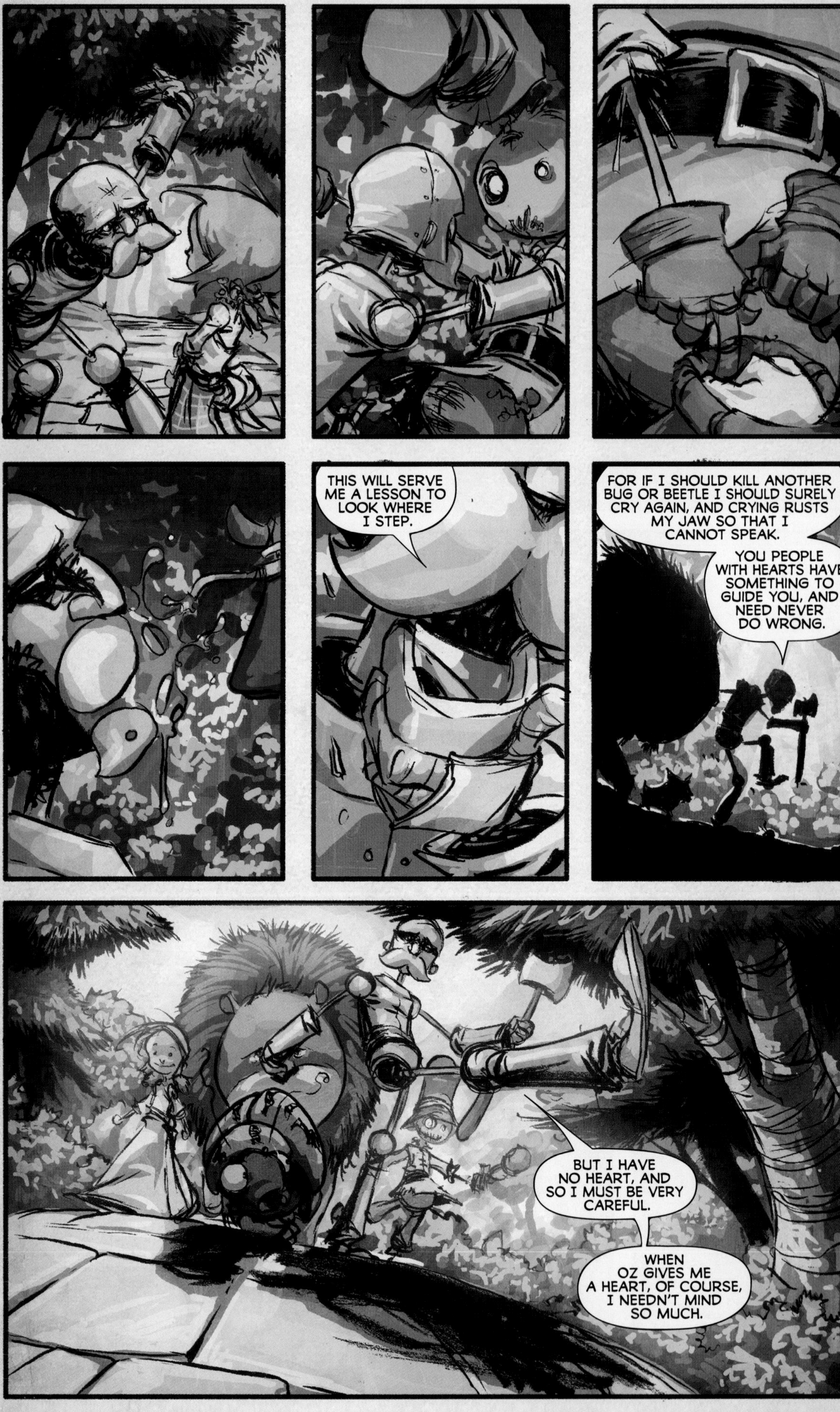
THIS WILL SERVE ME A LESSON TO LOOK WHERE I STEP.
FOR IF I SHOULD KILL ANOTHER BUG OR BEETLE I SHOULD SURELY CRY AGAIN, AND CRYING RUSTS MY JAW SO THAT I CANNOT SPEAK.
YOU PEOPLE WITH HEARTS HAVE SOMETHING TO GUIDE YOU, AND NEED NEVER DO WRONG.
BUT I HAVE NO HEART, AND SO I MUST BE VERY CAREFUL.
WHEN OZ GIVES ME A HEART, OF COURSE, I NEEDN'T MIND SO MUCH.